Puppy Tales

EMILY

Manufactured in U.S.A. for the
publishers Peter Haddock Ltd.
Bridlington, England.

ISBN: 0 7105 0898 0

Cover Illustration by Jon Goodell

Illustrations by Lisa Berrett,
Krista Brauckmann-Towns,
Jane Chambless Wright,
Drew-Brook-Cormack Associates,
Kate Sturman Gorman, Judith Dufour Love,
Ben Mahan, Anastasia Mitchell,
Anita Nelson, Rosario Valderrama

Two Little Dogs

Two little dogs sat by the fire,
　　Next to a pile of coal-dust,
When one dog said to the other dog,
　　"If you won't talk, why, I must."

My Dog Spot

I have a white dog
   Whose name is Spot,
And he's sometimes white
   And he's sometimes not.
But whether he's white
   Or whether he's not,
There's a patch on his ear
   That makes him Spot.

Where Has My Little Dog Gone?

Oh, where, oh, where has my little dog gone?
   Oh, where, oh, where can he be?
With his ears cut short and his tail cut long,
   Oh, where, oh, where can he be?

Bow-Wow

Bow-wow, says the dog;
   Mew-mew, says the cat;
Grunt, grunt, goes the hog;
   And squeak, goes the rat.

A fine song I have made,
   To please you, mummy dear;
And if it is well sung,
   'Twill be charming to hear.

Ride Away

Ride away, ride away, Johnny shall ride,
  And he shall have kitty cat tied to one side;
And he shall have little dog tied to the other;
  And Johnny shall ride to see his grandmother.

What Are Little Boys Made Of?

What are little boys made of, made of?
　　What are little boys made of?
Slugs and snails, and puppy-dogs' tails;
　　That's what little boys are made of, made of.

What are little girls made of, made of?
　　What are little girls made of?
Sugar and spice, and all things nice,
　　That's what little girls are made of, made of.

I'm Just a Little Puppy

I'm just a little puppy and as good as can be,
  And why they call me naughty I'm sure I cannot see,
I've only carried off one shoe and torn the baby's hat,
  And chased the ducks and spilled the milk—
    there's nothing bad in that!

Hark! Hark!

Hark, hark, the dogs do bark!
    Beggars are coming to town;
Some in jags, and some in rags,
    And some in velvet gown.

Mother Quack's Dog and Cat

Old Mother Quack
   Lived in a shack
Along with her dog and cat;
   What they ate I can't tell
But it's known very well
   That not one of the party was fat.

Old Mother Quack
   Scoured out her shack
And washed both her dog and cat;
   The cat scratched her nose,
And no one quite knows
   Who was the gainer by that?

Caesar's Song

Bow-wow-wow!
　　Whose dog art thou?
Little Tom Tinker's dog,
　　Bow-wow-wow!